I0741944
LUNDCLAR
Creative Productions LLC
Presents

Beararms Mckenzie and the Shreveport Aquarium
Text and illustrations copyright © 2018
Lunisolar Creative Productions, L.L.C.
All rights reserved. No part of this book may be reproduced
or utilized in any form or by any means, electronic or
mechanical, including photocopying, recording, or by any
information storage and retrieval system, without written
permission from the publisher.

Lunisolar Creative Productions, L.L.C.
Shreveport, LA 71118
LunisolarCreativeProductions.com
Beararmsmckenzie.com

Written by: Katie Baten
Illustrations by: Will Baten
Edited by: Caitlin Sattler

Beararms McKenzie and the Shreveport Aquarium

THE SHREVEPORT AQUARIUM

Exit
Eels!
Large tanks where the Triggerfish are
The tunnel with the sharks
Pacific Northwest Shoreline Touch Pool
Real Coral!
Spider Crabs!
Sea Jellies!
Stingrays!
Entrance
Dogfaced Puffer & French Angelfish
Arboretum

As the McKenzie spaceship began it*s decent into Louisiana airspace, Beararms was bubbling with anticipation for his return to Earth.

He was very excited to discover new things.

Beararms had learned of a place called the Shreveport Aquarium, and he desperately wanted to visit. He was told there would be all kinds of new creatures to see and touch. Ragna, his sister, was a very important scientist in his world, the Kingdom in the Sky, and she was accompanying him on this journey.

hreveport
Aquarium

When they arrived at the aquarium, they had a hard time containing their excitement. They proudly presented their tickets and proceeded through the doorway to explore.

Beararms and Ragna were mesmerized as they entered a corridor with two large tanks of water on each side. Many peculiar creatures glided through the watery enclosure.

Since Beararms and Ragna were from another galaxy, they booked a special tour so they could learn as much as possible about the hundreds of animals in the aquarium. Their tour guide explained that the first tanks contained many different reef fish, such as blue tangs, emperor angelfish, triggerfish, foxface rabbitfish and parrotfish. Most of these "fin-tastic" fish could be found in the Indo-Pacific region, which was far away from Louisiana.

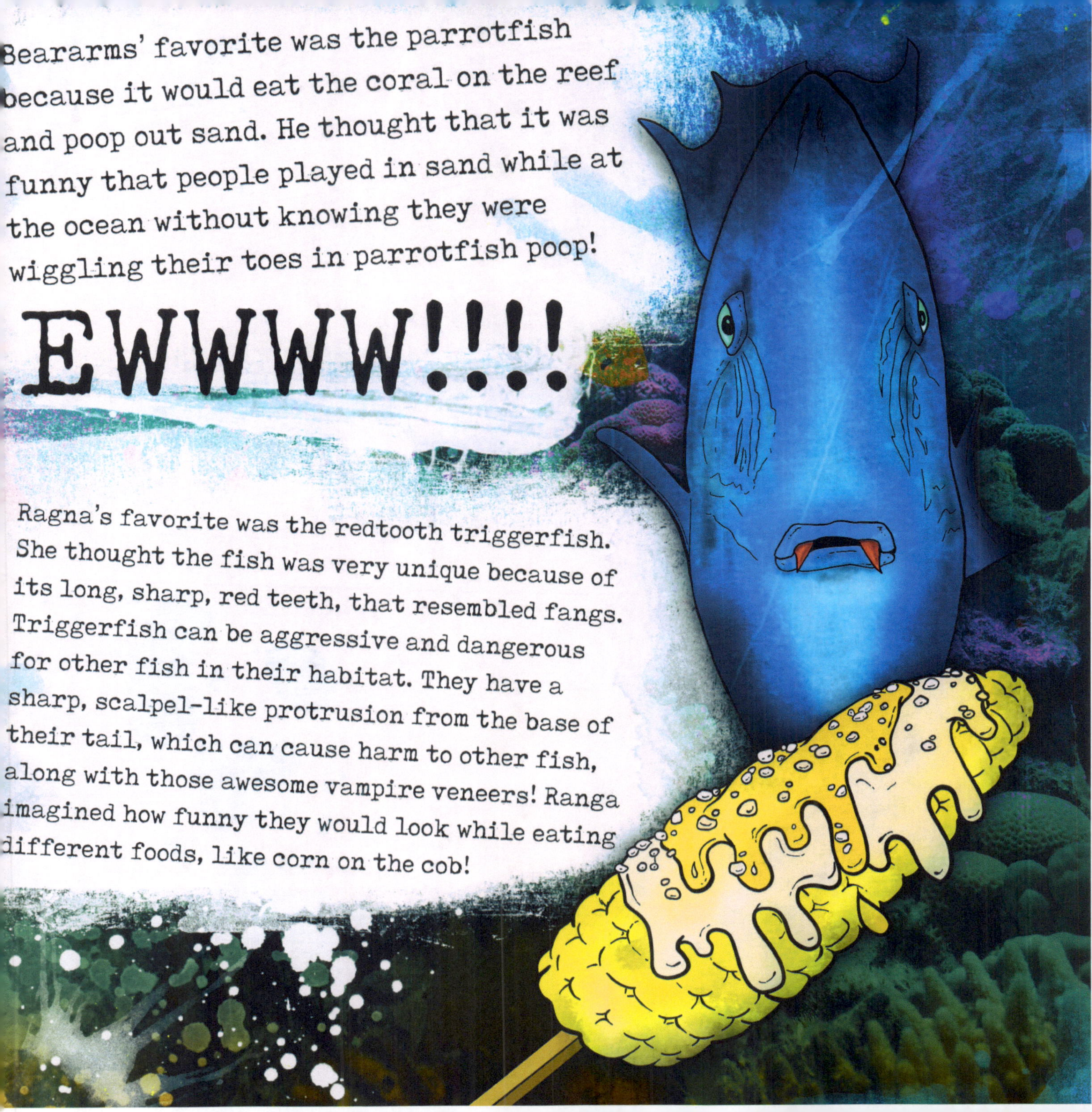

Beararms' favorite was the parrotfish because it would eat the coral on the reef and poop out sand. He thought that it was funny that people played in sand while at the ocean without knowing they were wiggling their toes in parrotfish poop!

EWWWW!!!!

Ragna's favorite was the redtooth triggerfish. She thought the fish was very unique because of its long, sharp, red teeth, that resembled fangs. Triggerfish can be aggressive and dangerous for other fish in their habitat. They have a sharp, scalpel-like protrusion from the base of their tail, which can cause harm to other fish, along with those awesome vampire veneers! Ranga imagined how funny they would look while eating different foods, like corn on the cob!

reefs·cities in the sea

The next space has several smaller tanks,
each with its own unique set of sea animals.
The French angelfish caught Beararms' eye.

The French angelfish was a great help to its tank. By cleaning up debris and parasites off of other fish, the French angel has created a symbiotic relationship with its tank mates. Even the fish that would normally want to eat the French angel would not do so because it was such a great cleaner!

Beararms and Ragna were both drawn to one very peculiar fish, the dogface puffer.

The fish itself had a very odd shape, with large eyes and tiny fins. It has a beak-like mouth, which Ragna thought was unusual for a fish. They learned that the puffer could suck in water, causing its body to inflate like a beach ball! It did this if it felt threatened by another creature.

The weird, beak-like mouth was actually a set of teeth that keeps growing throughout the puffer's life. Like a beaver's teeth, the puffer's teeth needed to be filed down so it would not continue to grow. The biologists at the Aquarium would feed them special food for this purpose. The dogface puffer is actually a very smart fish. It could even recognize the shirts the staff members wear. So when feeding time came, it would come right up to the front of the tank, ready to eat.

As they continued following the flow of people making their way through the exhibits, they entered a large, greenhouse-like area called the Arboretum. This was a very special area because everything contained in the Arboretum is indigenous to Louisiana, meaning you can find most of these species in your own backyard!

The wood ducks waddled around the foliage near a gently moving creek as the sun poured through the arboretum with a warm welcome. Beararms and Ragna made their way around the circular area until they reached the Community Tank.

Up until this point, all of the animals could be found in saltwater environments. The Community tank was different because its creatures could be found in the freshwater lakes of Caddo Parish.

Their guide pointed out a myriad of animals, including the humongous bottom-dwelling catfish, elusive alligator gar, darting white perch, and the amazing alligator snapping turtle!

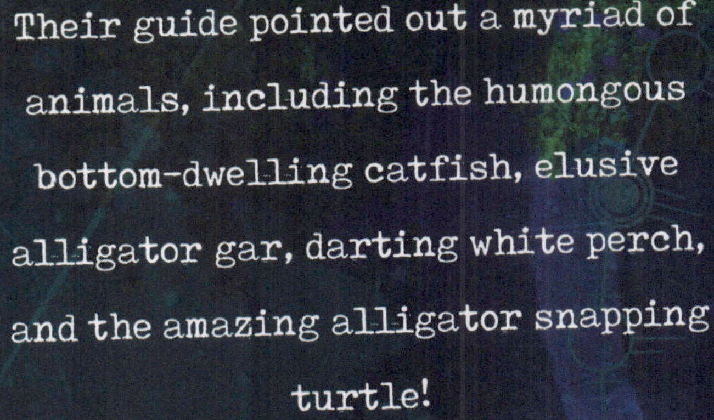

The alligator snapping turtle was drawing a large crowd of onlookers. It looked like an ancient creature with long claws protruding from its webbed feet.

It had a sharp, snub nose with beady eyes peering from inside its enclosure. The most interesting feature was its cumbersome yet very sharp shell that protected its body. The alligator snapping turtle is one of the largest freshwater turtles and closely resembles it pre-historic ancestors. That must be an oooooolllllllddd, grumpy dinosaur!

At last, Beararms and Ragna reached the first of three "touch stations" where they could interact with different creatures. The first touch area was modeled after the Pacific Northwest Shoreline off the coast of Oregon in the United States.

They made their way to a shallow pool containing sea stars, urchins, keyhole limpets and shiner fish. Beararms and Ragna carefully petted the sea stars, which were funny little creatures with five legs. They were spread out all through the shallow tank. Some were on the rocks, and some were on the sandy floor.

Ragna's favorite was the Ochre sea star. It was a large, purple sea star with five legs and short spines along its top. The Ochre sea star is very important to its habitat. The Ochres are a keystone species for their environment, meaning, if they were taken away, many other species may not survive. The very ecosystem would change drastically without their presence.

While this was an interesting fact, Ragna's favorite thing about the sea stars was their perseverance. Ochre sea stars are cleaver eaters. They can open the most tight-lipped clam with just two legs. The sea star would perch on top of clams and slowly apply pressure until the clam became tired and was unable to hold its shell closed.

It would then extract one of its two stomachs and drink the body of the clam for food.

What if YOUR stomach could come out of your body and eat things up?!

Way to go super star!!

GROSS!

Sea stars are also part of a group of special animals that may have the ability to be immortal, but Beararms and Ragna would find out more about that later.

Making their way out of the cold-water habitat of the North Pacific Shoreline, Beararms and Ragna entered the more relaxed environment of the reef.

The first thing they noticed was some unusual, snake-like being trying to communicate with him from inside the tank.

"Hey Ragna!" exclaimed Beararms. "What do you think they are trying to tell us?"

"I can't hear them through the tank!" said Beararms loudly.

The tour guide overheard Beararms' confusion and politely interrupted.

"They are not talking to you," the guide said. "Although it does look like that, these Tessalata, or honeycomb eels have to open their mouths in order to breathe." "Their gills are on the inside instead of on the outside of their body, like fish. So they have to open their mouths to get oxygen from the water to breathe. This makes it appear as though they are talking or yawning."

Beararms was disappointed. He would have been SO excited to go back to his home planet and brag about his new friend, the Earth eel. They were still fun to look at and quite peculiar as they wound themselves around the rocks and just slightly poked their heads out every now and then.

As soon as they left the eels, they entered
the coolest tunnel Beararms had ever been
in. There was glass everywhere! He felt
like he was inside the reef! All around him,
hundreds of fish swam past.

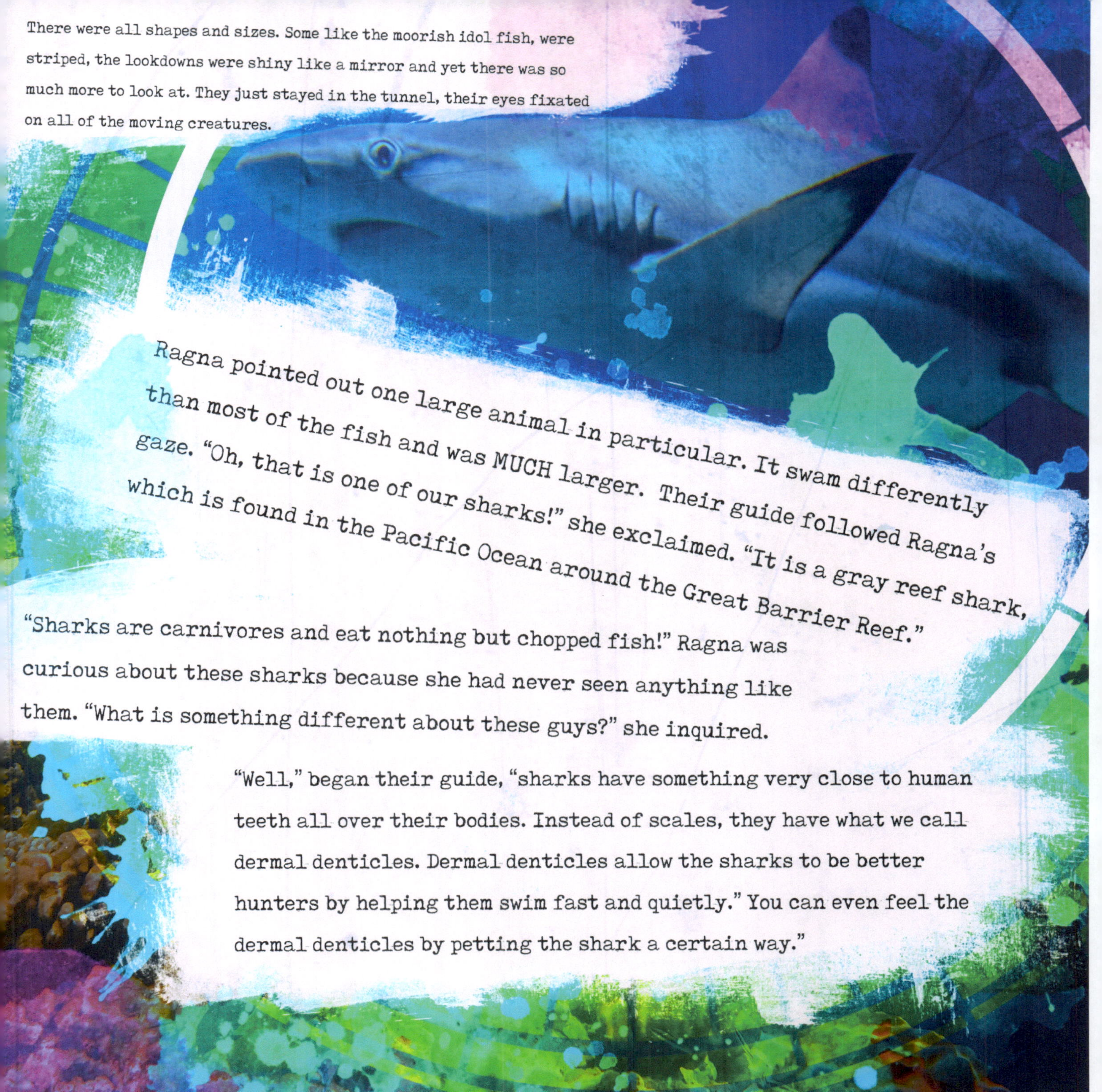

There were all shapes and sizes. Some like the moorish idol fish, were striped, the lookdowns were shiny like a mirror and yet there was so much more to look at. They just stayed in the tunnel, their eyes fixated on all of the moving creatures.

Ragna pointed out one large animal in particular. It swam differently than most of the fish and was MUCH larger. Their guide followed Ragna's gaze. "Oh, that is one of our sharks!" she exclaimed. "It is a gray reef shark, which is found in the Pacific Ocean around the Great Barrier Reef."

"Sharks are carnivores and eat nothing but chopped fish!" Ragna was curious about these sharks because she had never seen anything like them. "What is something different about these guys?" she inquired.

"Well," began their guide, "sharks have something very close to human teeth all over their bodies. Instead of scales, they have what we call dermal denticles. Dermal denticles allow the sharks to be better hunters by helping them swim fast and quietly." You can even feel the dermal denticles by petting the shark a certain way."

Beararms was not sure if he would like tiny teeth all of his body.

He much preferred his fur. After all, he did not think that dermal denticles would keep your feet warm, and he loved warm feet!

Beararms tuned back in as the guide said, "Okay one last thing, see if you can spot our humpnose unicornfish. It's a unicorn without a horn!"

Beararms wondered who stole its horn....

Next they walked into CONTACT COVE. Beararms thought this sounded like a place where supervillians might have their secret lair. Instead of another big tank, there was a giant pool in the middle of the room.

The guide led them to the shallow end of the pool. Beararms peeked over the edge and was amazed by all of the sleek animals that seemed to be floating or flying around the tank.

Inside the tank were four different species of rays. Most of them lived in Australia, but Beararms' favorite was the Cownose Ray that lived in the Florida Keys. He was told this was much closer than Australia.

The cownose rays were friendly and playful. The blue spot rays, black whiptail and reticulated whiptail rays, preferred to stay at the bottom of the tank.

When Beararms dipped his paw into the water, they quickly swam up to greet them. Bearams realized that if he touched them a certain way they felt rough, but if he brushed them the opposite direction, they felt smooth. Rays, like the sharks, also have dermal denticles, which is what gave them this unique texture. Beararms learned that the reason the cownose were so friendly was because in their natural habitat, they usually do not stay at the bottom of the ocean floor. They prefer to swim in the water column like their close relative, the manta ray.

Oh, and they LOVE food. They thought maybe Beararms had food, and they wanted to check to see if he did.

Ragna was confused. She had heard that stingrays were dangerous and would hurt people with their tail, when they are out in the wild. Their guide explained that rays are equipped with a barb, which is more like a human fingernail that is on their tail. In this tank, all of the rays got their barbs clipped to keep them from hurting each other or anyone else. Over time, their barbs will grow back, and they will have to be trimmed again.

Beararms noted a strange creature that looked like an armored tank moving slowly across the bottom of the tank. He raised his hand. "What is that?" he asked excitedly, pointing at the little brown object moving on the bottom.

"Well, those are the horseshoe crabs," replied the guide. "They are the cleaners for this tank. Stingrays are messy eaters, and the horseshoe crabs clean up all of the debris, making the tank cleaner for everyone."

Beararms was surprised by how dirty Earth sea creatures were. First, the reef fish needed the French angelfish, and now these rays need a crab. He did not think he would be assigned a special cleaner to help him out with his messes. This made him a little jealous of the rays.

They moved on to a smaller pool with the most unique little creatures. They were bright red or orange with striking white stripes. They had several antennae, kind of like Ragna, and small, wispy legs.

"These are the cleaner shrimp. They are also nature's helpers. They love to clean dead skin, wounds, and other foreign particles off of anything that comes in their way. The shrimp and the moray eel have a symbiotic relationship, amongst others." The guide showed them how to dip their palms into the water and allow the shrimp climb into your open palm. Beararms watched as people placed their open palms in the shallow water. One or two shrimp would slowly gather by each hand and proceed to clean under their fingernails or on their skin.

Beararms wanted to try. He gingerly lowered his palm into the water. ZOOM, WHAM. ALL of the cleaner shrimp in the tank rushed over and began attending to his paw. All. Of. Them.

Beararms looked around sheepishly. "I wash my hands!" he said, as he shot a look at Ragna, who was gazing at him with disapproval.

A little embarrassed by the cleaner shrimp incident, Beararms decided to make his way into the next room.

He and Ragna proceeded though the doorway into an ethereal, relaxing blue room. Mesmerizing, glowing creatures seemed to float through the water with little to no effort. Ragna found an opening to one of the tanks. She was able to stand inside and see the curious creatures from all angles. She loved being surrounded by these elusive, transparent objects.

She heard their tour guide speaking through the tank. She decided to slip out and find out just what these guys were.

"Comb Jellies," their guide was saying and pointing at the tank Ragna had just emerged from. Beararms looked confused. "What's wrong?" asked Ragna. "Is that where jelly comes from?" whispered Beararms. "No Beararms! Comb Jellies, not PEANUT BUTTER AND JELLY FISH," replied Ragna.

"Comb Jellies are bioluminescent jellies that are actually classified as Ctenophora, which are different than jellyfish people usually think about. Ctenophora do not have stinging cells. Instead they have sticky tentacles."

"The cool thing about these guys, as well as our next amazing animal, is they have these special cells in their bodies that allow them to regenerate legs, tentacles, and sometimes even parts of their main body. These cells can be used to regenerate anything they might need."

Ragna thought this was so cool. She remembered that sea stars, as well as cephalopods, crustaceans, and now Comb Jellies were apart of this immortal animal group. What could be cooler than re-growing your own body parts?

"And now" announced their guide, " on to my favorite sea creature, the Japanese spider crab!"

"Oh, wow," said Beararms out loud. "These things are so WEIRD!" Ragna nudged him and motioned for him to be quiet. "Sorry, they are just the biggest crabs I've ever seen on this planet," Beararms whispered loudly.

"Why, yes they are!" said their guide. "These fascinating crustaceans live in the deep waters off of Japan. So deep in fact, they barely see light throughout their lifetime, which can be 100 or more years!"

Beararms shot his paw up. "What do they eat?" he asked excitedly. He was very curious now and had moved as close to the tank as possible.

"Spider crabs are scavengers and move around on the ocean floor until they find something that has already died. They will eat until they can't eat anymore," replied their guide.

"I bet these guys would make a great pet," Beararms said to Ragna as they moved past the tank. "Didn't you hear the guide Beararms? Those crabs can get as big as 12ft from leg to leg, and their bodies are too heavy for shallow waters! We don't have a tank big enough for that! "Ragna replied.

Beararms and Ragna lingered a little longer at the last tank. It was small, but beautiful. Their guide was still nearby, so Ragna decided to pull him over and ask a few more questions.

"What is this? It is so pretty."

"Why, this is a coral reef," he explained. "Coral is also a somewhat immortal species. They can reproduce more coral just by fragmenting."

"There are so many different kinds," mused Ragna. "Actually," began the guide, "there are less than you may think. Recent genotyping has shown us that the same species of coral can look different when living at a different depth."

"Coral reefs are a keystone species for their ecosystem. Some coral are even more aggressive than others. They will sometimes fight for space by deploying sweeper tentacles if the reef gets too crowded. We learn new things about coral every day!"

"How fascinating," mused Ragna. She was about to ask another question when Beararms interrupted. "I am SO hungry. Let's go eat!"

Ragna thanked their guide and they
went to find some food. "That was SO
MUCH FUN!" Beararms yelled loudly.

"We need to come back soon!"
Ragna agreed.
"It's worth the trip!"

The END

Glossary:

Australia: The smallest continent between the Indian Ocean and the southwest Pacific Ocean.

Barb: A sharp projection.

Bioluminescent: The biochemical emission of light by living organisms.

Carnivores: Any animal that eats meat.

Cells: Are known as the building blocks of life. Cells are the smallest structural unit of an organism or in this case, animal.

Cephalopod: Any marine mollusk with a well-developed head and eyes. Includes, octopuses, squids and cuttlefish.

Coral Reef: Is a ridge of rock in the sea that is formed by the deposit and growth of coral.

Crustacean: Characterized as a large arthropod with an exoskeleton, segmented body and jointed appendages. Most common are lobsters and crabs.

Ctenophores (pronounced Teno-for): is an aquatic invertebrate, like the comb jellyfish.

Dermal Denticles: Tiny V-shaped scales that cover the body of sharks and rays. They are more like teeth than fish scales.

Ecosystem: A biological community of interacting organisms and their physical environment.

Fragmenting: Deliberate acts by coral to propagate a reef, so they can get bigger.

Freshwater: Of, or found in freshwater, not in the sea.

Genotyping: To investigate the genetic makeup of an organism.

Gills: Allows fish to breathe underwater by extracting oxygen from water that flows over the surface of the gill.

Great Barrier Reef: The largest living reef on Earth. Located off of the coast of Queensland in Australia.

Habitat: Natural home or environment of an animal, plant or organism.

Indigenous: Originating or occurring naturally in a particular place, native to an area.

Immortal: Live forever.

Indo-Pacific: The maritime space across the Indian Ocean and western Pacific Ocean to East Asia.

Keystone Species: A species in which other species in an ecosystem largely depend upon, such that if it were removed the ecosystem would drastically change.

Manta Ray: A large ray that lives in warm seas and has fins that look like wings.

Rays: Marine animals with a flattened body and eyes on the upper surface. Usually referred to as stingrays or skates.

Reef: A ridge of jagged rock, coral or sand just above or below the surface of the sea.

Regenerate: To replace or regrow lost or injured tissue.

Saltwater: Composition of oceans.

Species: Closely related organisms that are similar to each other and can produce offspring.

Stinging cells: Cnidarians like jellyfish have stinging cells in their tentacles that are used to capture and stun prey.

Symbiotic: Denoting a mutual beneficial relationship between different organisms.

References / Contributors

https://www.pugetsound.edu/academics/academic-resources/
slater-museum/exhibits/marine-panel/ochre-sea-star/

https://www.arkive.org/alligator-snapping-turtle/macrochelys-temminckii/

Kimberly A. Lobit- Education Manager

Special Thanks to: Jessica Schiele at Cohab

Our other books! Collect them all!

LunisolarCreativeProductions.com
beararmsmckenzie.com

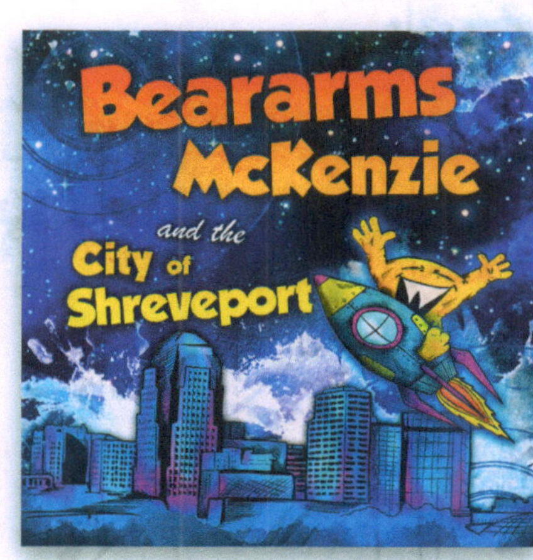

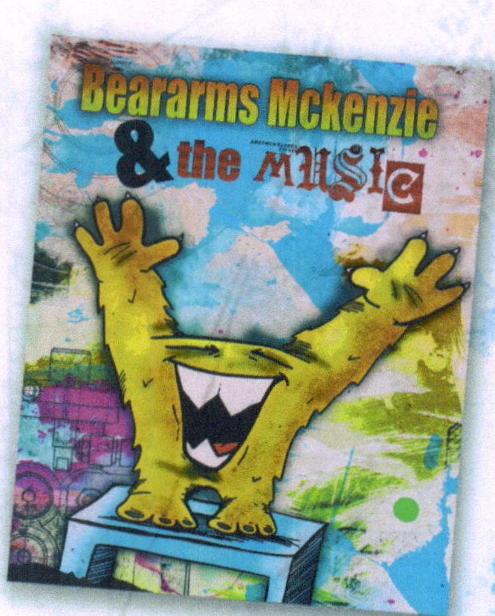